A Giant First-Start Reader

This easy reader contains only 49 different words, repeated often to help the young reader develop word recognition and interest in reading.

Basic word list for *Birthday Surprise*

a	hat	red
all	he	ring
alone	hears	room
and	hides	sadly
bed	his	Sammy
big	inside	says
birthday	into	slowly
blue	is	sound
bow	it	surprise
box	likes	the
covers	me	to
door	my	today
gets	nobody	under
goes	on	very
green	opens	white
happy	party	yellow
	puts	

Birthday Surprise

Written by Louis Sabin

Illustrated by John Magine

Troll Associates

Library of Congress Cataloging in Publication Data

Sabin, Louis.
    Birthday surprise.

    Summary: Sammy is sad when no one seems to remember
his birthday.
    [1. Birthdays—Fiction]   I. Magine, John.   II. Title.
PZ7.S1173Bi   [E]   81-2632
ISBN 0-89375-527-3 (case)   AACR2
ISBN 0-89375-528-1 (pbk.)

Sammy is all alone.

"Nobody likes me," says Sammy
sadly.

"And today is my birthday," says
Sammy.
"Ring! Ring!"

Sammy gets a big, red box.

He opens the bow.

Sammy opens the box.

Inside is a big, white box.

Sammy opens the box.

Inside is a green box.

Sammy opens the box.

Inside is a red box.

Sammy opens the box.

Inside is a blue box.

Sammy opens the box.

Inside is a yellow box.

Inside is a party hat.

The hat is red, white and blue.

Sammy puts it on.

"Happy Birthday to me," he says sadly.

Sammy goes to his room.

He gets into bed.

Sammy hears a sound.
The door opens slowly.

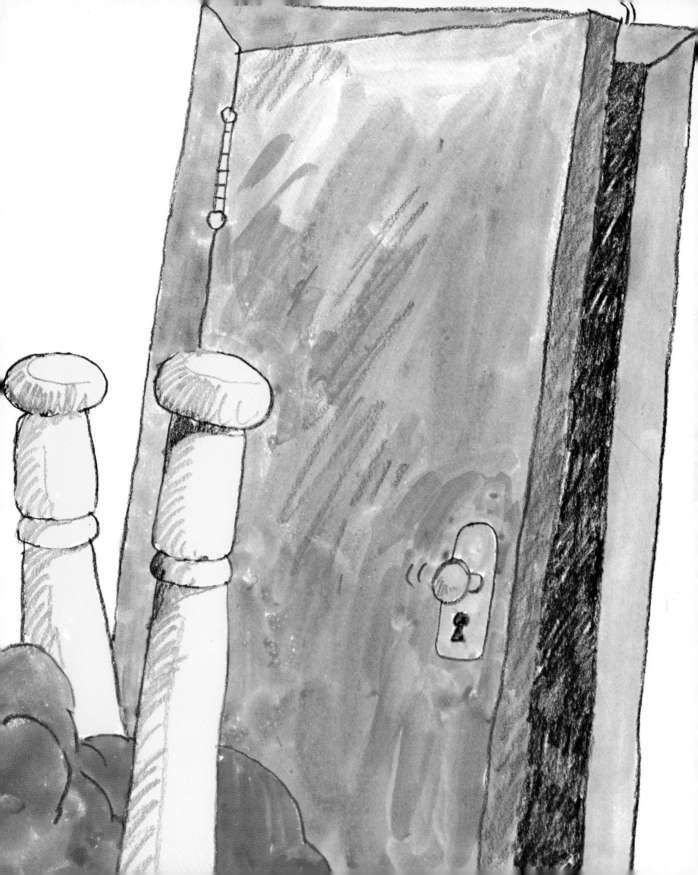

He hides under the covers.

"Happy Birthday, Sammy!"

"Happy Birthday. It is a very happy birthday!" says Sammy.